The GRASSHOPPER and the ANTS

Debra J. Housel

Editorial Director
Dona Herweck Rice

Assistant Editor
Leslie Huber, M.A.

Editor-in-Chief
Sharon Coan, M.S.Ed.

Editorial Manager
Gisela Lee, M.A.

Creative Director
Lee Aucoin

Illustration Manager/Designer
Timothy J. Bradley

Illustrator
Chad Thompson

Publisher
Rachelle Cracchiolo, M.S.Ed.

Teacher Created Materials
5301 Oceanus Drive
Huntington Beach, CA 92649-1030
http://www.tcmpub.com
ISBN 978-1-4333-0292-3
©2009 Teacher Created Materials, Inc.
Printed in China
Nordica.052018.CA21800433

The Grasshopper and the Ants

Story Summary

The grasshopper makes music all summer long while the ants find and store food. The grasshopper laughs at them and tells them to play instead.

The ants warn the grasshopper that winter is coming. They keep on working. When winter does come, the ants are warm and well fed. The grasshopper is cold and hungry.

What will become of the grasshopper? Read the story to find out.

Tips for Performing Reader's Theater

Adapted from Aaron Shepard

- Don't let your script hide your face. If you can't see the audience, your script is too high.

- Look up often when you speak. Don't just look at your script.

- Talk slowly, so the audience knows what you are saying.

- Talk loudly, so everyone can hear you.

- Talk with feelings. If the character is sad, let your voice be sad. If the character is surprised, let your voice be surprised.

- Stand up straight. Keep your hands and feet still.

- Remember that even when you are not talking, you are still your character.

- Narrator, be sure to give the characters enough time for their lines.

Tips for Performing
Reader's Theater *(cont.)*

- If the audience laughs, wait for them to stop before you speak again.

- If someone in the audience talks, don't pay attention.

- If someone walks into the room, don't pay attention.

- If you make a mistake, pretend it was right.

- If you drop something, try to leave it where it is until the audience is looking somewhere else.

- If a reader forgets to read his or her part, see if you can read the part instead, make something up, or just skip over it. Don't whisper to the reader!

- If a reader falls down during the performance, pretend it didn't happen.

The Grasshopper and the Ants

Characters

Narrator 1	Ant 1
Narrator 2	Ant 2
Queen Ant	**Grasshopper**

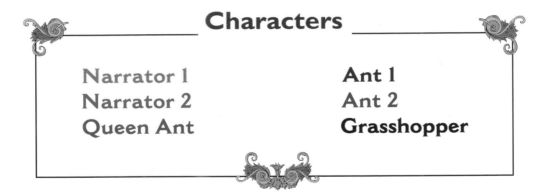

Setting

This reader's theater takes place in a grassy field during the summer and winter.

Act 1

Narrator 1:	There is a large colony of ants that lives in an anthill in a grassy field.
Narrator 2:	The ants wake every day at dawn.
Queen Ant:	Oh, just look at that lovely sunrise!
Ant 1:	Let's get to work!
Ant 2:	We must find food to store in our anthill.
Narrator 1:	The ants live inside the anthill. It looks like a sandy mound with a hole in the top.
Narrator 2:	They spend every day searching for food.
Ant 1:	I've found some tasty bread crumbs.

Ant 2:   See this yummy dead insect!

Narrator 1:   The ants carry food piece by piece back to their anthill.

Narrator 2:   Although they move slowly under the weight of their burdens, the ants never stop.

Queen Ant: I am pleased with all the food you have found. Now store it here, under the ground.

Ant 1:   We'll go search for more tasty morsels, my queen.

Ant 2:   Even though the sun is hot, we don't mind working. This way we will have all that we need when the winter winds blow.

Narrator 1:   In this same field lives a lazy grasshopper that sleeps until noon each day.

Narrator 2: The grasshopper spends every day making music by rubbing its hind legs against its front wings.

Grasshopper: It feels good to be alive! I love to make music.

Narrator 1: The grasshopper finds food easily, for it eats anything green. It especially enjoys leaves.

Narrator 2: One day the grasshopper notices the ants returning to their anthill. Each one of them carries a heavy load.

Grasshopper: What are you doing?

Ant 1: We are gathering food to store underground.

Ant 2: We spend every day collecting tidbits of food.

Grasshopper: Why do you work so hard? There is plenty of food around! I am never hungry.

Ant 1:   Yes, there is plenty of food right now. But in time the days will grow colder and shorter.

Ant 2:   Summer will turn to fall, and we must be ready. That's why we gather food now.

Grasshopper: You silly ants! Enjoy yourselves!

Ant 1:   Silly? We are really quite smart, thank you!

Ant 2:   We must work now so that we will have food during the winter.

Grasshopper: You work in the hot sun when you should sing and dance. That is what I do each day.

Narrator 1:   The ants do not respond.

Narrator 2:   They don't want to waste time arguing with the grasshopper.

Grasshopper: Don't you know that summer is playtime?

Poem: Grasshopper Green

Act 2

Narrator 1:   The ants enter their cozy anthill. Other busy ants fill the passageways.

Narrator 2:   Some ants are cleaning and feeding the queen. Others care for the eggs and feed the newly hatched larvae.

Narrator 1:   The hardworking ants put their food into storage.

Queen Ant: Would you like to work inside the anthill today?

Ant 1:   No, thank you. I prefer working outside.

Ant 2:   I don't mind carrying heavy loads.

Ant 1:   Besides, we do not want to give that insect the satisfaction.

Queen Ant: What do you mean?

Ant 2:   We met a big, green, and very rude bug.

Ant 1:   It called us silly for working.

Queen Ant: Did the insect rub its legs and wings to make music?

Ant 2:   That's right! How did you know?

Queen Ant: That is a grasshopper. Grasshoppers are lazy. They only leap about and make music.

Ant 1: We said that we had to work now to eat later. The grasshopper said that it is never hungry.

Queen Ant: Of course it is not hungry now. It is summer! But when winter comes, the grasshopper will learn what hunger means.

Act 3

Narrator 1: The ants return to their work. Day after day, they leave the anthill soon after daybreak.

Narrator 2: They gather morsels all day. They never stop working until it is dusk.

Ant 1:   Oh, that grasshopper! It makes fun of us.

Ant 2:   It calls us silly and foolish.

Ant 1:   Why does it think life is all play?

Ant 2:   I don't know. But I do know this. When the grasshopper is cold and hungry this winter, I will laugh!

Grasshopper: There go the busy little ants. Work, work, work! So silly!

Ant 1:   We only stop when it rains. Then we stay inside until the weather improves.

Ant 2:   We are not silly. By the time you see just how clever we are, it will be too late.

Grasshopper: Too late for what?

Ant 1: Too late for you!

Ant 2: You'll die of cold and hunger this winter.

Grasshopper: No, I won't. There's plenty of food to go around.

Ant 1: That's true right now . . .

Ant 2: . . . but it won't always be so. Winter is coming!

Grasshopper: Oh, come on and play! You act like soldiers, marching and marching all day long.

Song: The Ants Go Marching

Act 4

Narrator 1: The days grow shorter and the nights grow longer.

Narrator 2: The nights turn sharply colder, but the ants do not stop their work. In fact, they just work harder and faster.

Grasshopper: Don't you ever rest? Come out of the sun and listen to my music.

Ant 1: It won't be summer much longer. Haven't you noticed how much shorter the days are?

Ant 2: Winter's around the corner. Haven't you felt how chilly it gets at night?

Grasshopper: Yes, but who cares? Summer is still here!

Ant 1: I am warning you. You should store food.

Ant 2:   All the green plants will die, and snow will cover everything. You will freeze or starve!

Grasshopper: I'm not worried!

Ant 1:   When the first snow falls, it will be too late. All green things die with the first frost.

Ant 2:   Winter lasts a long, long time. Months will pass before the green things grow again.

Narrator 1:   But the grasshopper just laughs and makes more music.

Narrator 2:   Just days later, winter arrives with a blast of cold air.

Narrator 1:   Ice crystals shine on the blades of grass. The ants are well prepared.

Narrator 2: They do not go out into the cold. They stay snug and warm inside their anthill.

Act 5

Narrator 1: It rains for many days. But one day when the rain breaks, the ants come out of their hill.

Narrator 2: They bring out some food that had gotten damp. They spread it out to dry.

Ant 1: Here comes the pesky grasshopper that made fun of us all summer.

Ant 2: I wonder what it wants.

Narrator 1: The grasshopper is nearly frozen.

Narrator 2: It had tried to keep warm huddled under some fallen leaves.

Narrator 1:	How the grasshopper wishes it had listened to the ants!
Narrator 2:	The grasshopper runs to the anthill.
Grasshopper:	I am so glad to see you! I am very hungry. Will you please share your food with me?
Ant 1:	Why should we?
Ant 2:	You laughed at us! Where is your food supply?
Grasshopper:	I did not gather any food. I spent the whole summer making music.
Ant 1:	Then you deserve to be hungry.
Ant 2:	Let's see how warm your music keeps you.
Queen Ant:	What is going on here?

Ant 1: This grasshopper wants us to share our food!

Ant 2: The grasshopper spent the summer laughing at us!

Queen Ant: Even so, it is unkind to let the grasshopper starve.

Ant 1: You mean you want us to share our food?

Ant 2: Are you sure we have enough?

Queen Ant: I am quite sure. But give the grasshopper just enough food to survive.

Grasshopper: Oh, thank you! Thank you so much! I am so hungry.

Queen Ant: I hope you have learned your lesson.

Grasshopper: Oh, I have! I have!

Ant 1: What have you learned?

Grasshopper: It is wise to plan for the future. Work today to eat tomorrow.

Queen Ant: It's always best to plan ahead.

Ant 2: That's for sure. And never laugh at us again!

Grasshopper: I won't! Please forgive me for laughing at you. I promise that I will never do it again. And, like you, I will plan for next winter.

All Ants: Now you're playing the right tune!

Grasshopper Green

Traditional

Grasshopper Green is a comical chap:
He lives on the best of fare.
Bright little trousers, jacket, and cap,
These are his summer wear.
Out in the meadow he loves to go,
Playing all day in the sun;
It's hopperty, skipperty, high and low,
Summer's the time for fun.

Grasshopper Green has a quaint little house;
It's in a field thick with hay.
Grandmother Spider, as still as a mouse,
Watches him over the way.
Gladly he's calling the children, I know,
Out in the beautiful sun;
It's hopperty, skipperty, high and low,
Summer's the time for fun.

 # The Ants Go Marching
Traditional

The ants go marching one by one, hurrah, hurrah!
The ants go marching one by one, hurrah, hurrah!
The ants go marching one by one.
The little one stops to suck his thumb.
And they all go marching down to the ground
To get out of the rain, boom, boom, boom!

The ants go marching two by two, hurrah, hurrah!
The ants go marching two by two, hurrah, hurrah!
The ants go marching two by two.
The little one stops to tie his shoe.
And they all go marching down to the ground
To get out of the rain, boom, boom, boom!

. . . The ants go marching three by three.
The little one stops to climb a tree.

. . . The ants go marching four by four.
The little one stops to shut the door.

Glossary

burdens—loads

chap—boy; fellow

colony—group that lives together

comical—funny

dusk—twilight; the time of day when the light fades into darkness

fare—food

huddled—crouched

larvae—newly hatched insects that slowly change into their adult form

morsels—tiny scraps of food

pesky—troublesome; bothersome

quaint—charming; old-fashioned

trousers—pants